OVER AT THE CASTLE

By BONI ASHBURN

ILLUSTRATED BY KELLY MURPHY

ABRAMS BOOKS FOR YOUNG READERS, NEW YORK

The illustrations in this book were made with
acrylic, oil, and gel medium on paper.

Library of Congress Cataloging-in-Publication Data

Ashburn, Boni.
Over at the castle / by Boni Ashburn ; illustrated by Kelly Murphy.
p. cm.
Summary: In this variation on the folk song "Over the Meadow," the occupants of a
medieval castle spend their day spinning, cleaning, cooking, and dancing, until they
receive a special surprise from their dragon neighbors.
ISBN 978-0-8109-8414-1
[1. Stories in rhyme. 2. Castles—Fiction. 3. Dragons—Fiction. 4.
Middle ages—Fiction. 5. Counting.] I. Murphy, Kelly, 1977– ill. II. Title.
PZ8.3.A737Ov 2010
[E]—dc22
2009023012

Text copyright © 2010 Boni Ashburn
Illustrations copyright © 2010 Kelly Murphy

Book design by Chad W. Beckerman

Printed and bound in China
10 9 8 7 6 5 4 3 2

Abrams Books for Young Readers are available at special discounts when purchased in quantity for
premiums and promotions as well as fundraising or educational use. Special editions can also be created
to specification. For details, contact specialmarkets@abramsbooks.com or the address below.

ABRAMS
THE ART OF BOOKS SINCE 1949

115 West 18th Street
New York, NY 10011
www.abramsbooks.com

To Matthew
(thanks for making dinner!)
—B. A.

For my trusty brother Jim
—K. M.

Over at the castle, on the hill in the sun,

Sit the old mother dragon and her little dragon one.

"Patience!" says the mother. "Okay," says the one.

So they laze all day on the hill in the sun.

Over at the castle, by the moat shining blue,

Stand the old gruff guard and his fellow guards two.

"Watch!" says the guard. "We watch!" say the two.

So they guard all day by the moat shining blue.

Over at the castle, by the old willow tree,

Play the carefree lord and his little lords three.

"Romp!" says the lord. "En garde!" say the three.

So they play all day by the old willow tree.

"Now?" begs little dragon. "Not yet!" says his mother.
So they laze the day away, a day like any other.

Over at the castle, doing chore after chore,

Work the old trusty servant and her helper servants four.

"Hustle!" says the servant. "We hustle!" say the four.

So they work all day doing chore after chore.

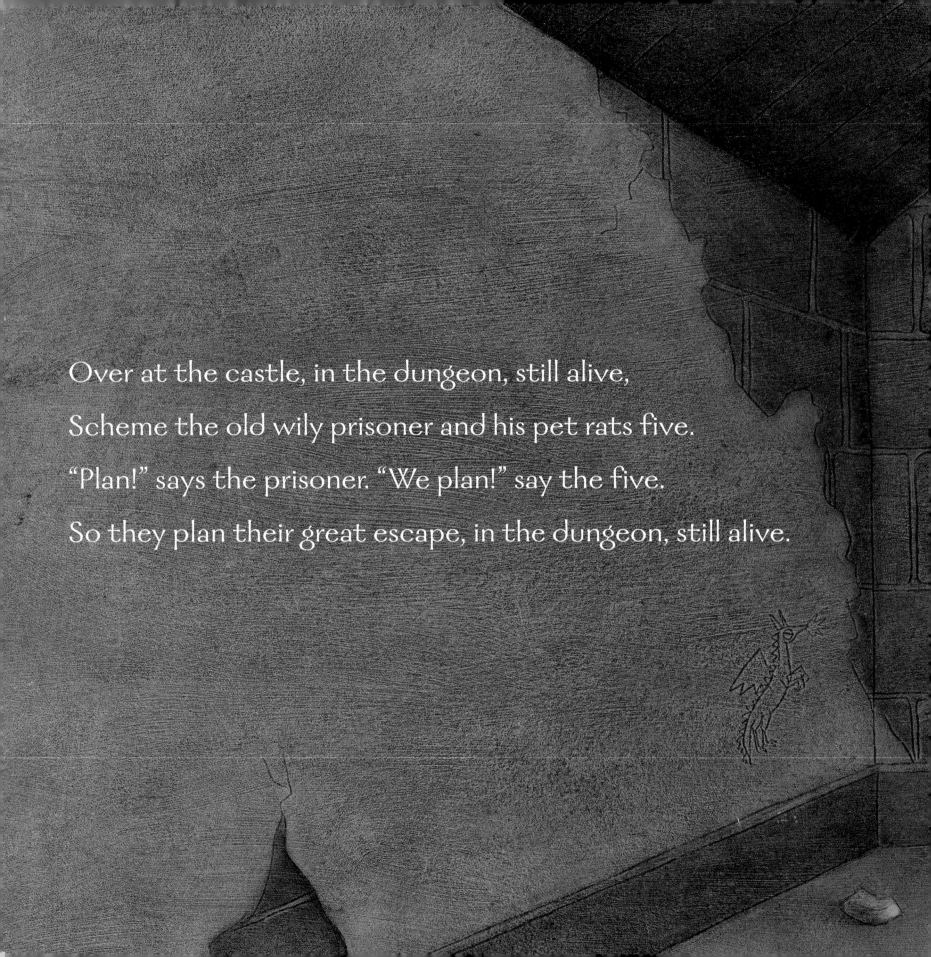

Over at the castle, in the dungeon, still alive,

Scheme the old wily prisoner and his pet rats five.

"Plan!" says the prisoner. "We plan!" say the five.

So they plan their great escape, in the dungeon, still alive.

Over at the castle, in the kitchen built of bricks,

Cook the old master chef and her sous chefs six.

"Sauté!" says the chef. "Flambé!" say the six.

So they cook all day in the kitchen built of bricks.

Over at the castle, in a tower up to heaven,

Toil the old woman weaver and her little weavers seven.

"Spin!" says the woman. "We spin!" say the seven.

So they spin all day in the tower up to heaven.

"Now?" begs little dragon. "Not yet!" says his mother.
So they laze the day away, a day like any other.

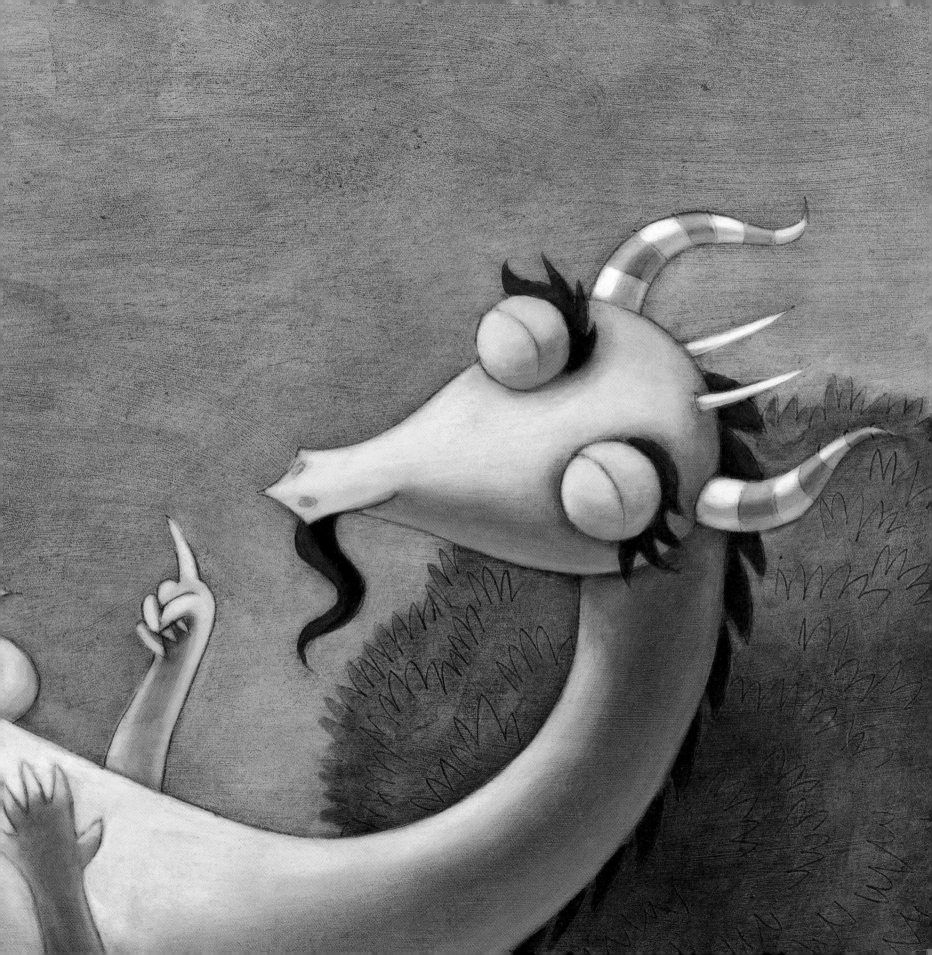

Over at the castle, in the hall grand and great,

Dance the guests at the party, a festive group of eight.

"Eat and drink!" says the lord. "Be merry!" cry the eight.

So they dance, eat, and drink in the hall grand and great.

Over at the castle, brave and strong, in a line,

Stand the knights in shining armor while they wait—all nine.

"Ready?" asks the leader. "We're ready!" say the nine.

And they wait . . . and they wait . . . mostly ready in a line.

Over at the castle, for the bored and waiting men,

Jesters juggle and perform—entertainers, all ten.

"More!" say the men. "Like this?" say the ten,

Who juggle and perform for the battle-ready men.

Over at the castle, under clear, dark skies,

All the weary people rest and heave great sighs.

They gaze out their windows with drowsy eyes

As the castle yawns under clear, dark skies.

Then . . .

"Flame?" begs little dragon. "Flame!" says his mother.

Then . . . WHOOOOOOOOOSHHHHHH!

And then another . . .

"Oh, boy!" says little dragon to his beaming, proud mother
On this night at the castle, a night like any other.